Bantam Books in the Choose Your Own Adventure® Series
Ask your bookseller for the books you have missed

STOCK CAR CHAMPION

BY R. A. MONTGOMERY

ILLUSTRATED BY LESLIE MORRILL

BANTAM BOOKS

NEW YORK · TORONTO · LONDON · SYDNEY · AUCKLAND

This is a work of fiction. All the characters and events in this book are fictitious. Any resemblance to persons living or dead is purely coincidental.

RL 4, age 10 and up

STOCK CAR CHAMPION
A Bantam Book / December 1989

CHOOSE YOUR OWN ADVENTURE® is a registered trademark of Bantam Books, a division of Bantam Doubleday Dell Publishing Group, Inc. Registered in U.S. Patent and Trademark Office and elsewhere.

Original conception of Edward Parkard

Cover art by Thierry Thompson
Interior illustrations by Leslie Morrill

ISBN 0-553-28294-8

Published simultaneously in the United States and Canada

Bantam Books are published by Bantam Books, a division of Bantam Doubleday Dell Publishing Group, Inc. Its trademark, consisting of the words "Bantam Books" and the portrayal of a rooster, is Registered in U.S. Patent and Trademark Office and in other countries. Marca Registrada. Bantam Books, 666 Fifth Avenue, New York, New York 10103.

PRINTED IN THE UNITED STATES OF AMERICA

OPM   0 9 8 7 6 5 4 3

STOCK CAR CHAMPION

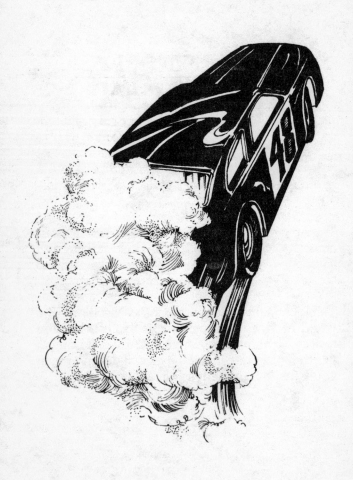

WARNING!!!

Do not read this book straight through from beginning to end. These pages contain many different adventures that you may have on your way to becoming a stock car racer. From time to time as you read along, you will be asked to make a choice. Your choice may lead to success or disaster!

The adventures you have are the results of your choices. You are responsible because you choose! After you make a choice, follow the instructions to see what happens to you next.

Think carefully before you make a decision. The world of stock car racing can be fun, but the racetrack can also be dangerous. Even if you get the chance to ride in the big race, it doesn't mean you'll make it to the finish line!

Good luck!

"I quit!" Bill Mazzaro yells, slamming down his wrench. "And furthermore, I never want to see you again." With that he turns around and storms out of the garage.

It is a bright, early June day in northern Vermont. A few clouds float by in the almost perfect blue sky. You look up waiting for Mike Peterson's response, but it doesn't take long.

"Good riddance," Mike says. "I wouldn't have you working on my car if you were the last mechanic on earth."

Mike Peterson owns a Massey Ferguson and Fiat tractor dealership. He is also one of the best NASCAR drivers in the Flying Tiger Class. For the past ten years Bill Mazzaro has been working with Mike as his mechanic. This year they are hoping to win the division championship.

You have always loved stock car racing, and you, too, dream of someday winning the trophy for the Flying Tiger division. You have worked with Mike and Bill as their apprentice for the last three years, helping in any way you can, from running errands and sweeping up to finally getting to work on the engines themselves.

In the time Bill and Mike worked together, they had become very close. Almost like brothers. But for the past six months you have noticed some tension building between them, and you knew that one day soon things would come to a head. You just didn't expect it *today*. It's the beginning of the racing season, and the first race is only a week away.

Turn to page 2.

2

You know that Mike has noticed how on edge Bill has been lately. Several times he's had to remind Bill who's boss. And you know what the problem has been all along. Bill wants to share some of the glory. He wants to either be a driver or at least get the credit that he feels he deserves. Bill feels that Mike ignores his efforts and contributions and doesn't recognize that a mechanic is indispensible, that without him there would be no race.

You're right in the middle of this misunderstanding. You personally like Bill and Mike, and they, in turn, like you. Together they have taught you all you know about maintaining and racing cars. In fact, just this spring, Mike Peterson had you out on the test track, practicing laps with him. He drove the new car, a Chevy Camaro 307 CID, and you drove last year's Buick 350 CID.

"You're a natural, kid," Mike had said after one long afternoon of racing around the track behind his dealership.

"Some day you'll be in the big race, and I don't mean the Flying Tiger Division. I mean the Indy 500!" Bill said.

Go on to the next page.

That made you feel great. It gave you the encouragement you needed to keep working as hard as you could toward your goal. All along you have benefitted from Mike's talent as a racer and Bill's mechanical abilities. But more than that, they have been good friends to you. Now, though, things have changed, and this perfect environment for learning—and friendship—has fallen apart.

Go on to the next page.

4

Bill Mazzaro stomps across the parking lot, lugging his tool chest with him. He places it in the back of the Ford Bronco 4 X 4, climbs in, and within seconds, screeches out of the lot.

Mike Peterson stands, his arms at his side, shaking his head. "Damn fool! I'm better off without him," he says, more to himself than to you. "Well, kid, I guess it's you and me. We're the team now. Driver and mechanic. How does that sound to you?"

"Whoa, thanks, Mike," you say. "But I can't be your mechanic. I mean, Bill's the best. I don't know enough yet."

"Hey, listen kid. You're talented. You have what it takes. Believe in yourself. Things got too *hot* for Bill—and now that he's no longer with us things just may get *hotter.* He's gone now, and you're my number one mechanic. Got it?"

Go on to the next page.

You nod, excited, but you feel nervous as well. Being chief mechanic for a stock car racer is a tough, important job loaded with responsibility—life-and-death responsibility. The driver's life depends not only on judgment and skill, but on his equipment as well. The mechanic is responsible for things like steering, suspension, tires, power plant, transmission—not to mention all the safety features like special roll bars, aircraft seat and shoulder belt harnesses, and safety windshields that pop out. Then there are the fuel cells in the tanks to prevent explosions, the fuel lines themselves, the springs and clutches, and on and on. And all of it must be maintained thoroughly and professionally. It's a lot for you to think of right now.

"I gotta go, Mike," you say. "I have algebra homework. Practice test before the finals. I'll see you later." You need to get out of there and think things through. Being chief mechanic is a challenge you have to think about first before you can make a commitment to Mike.

"Hey, I understand. Knock 'em dead, kid. I'll see you tomorrow. Remember: it's just you and me now."

Go on to the next page.

Your dirt bike isn't as fast as a stock car, but it can maneuver well, and in fifteen minutes you are back home at your grandfather's, where you will be living until your parents work out their problems. It's an old white farmhouse with an attached barn. Your grandfather used to be a dairy farmer, but he gave that up years ago and sold off the land as well as the cows. In the spring he sugars the maple trees, and in the summer he has a small but very successful nursery. There are some flowers, but mostly trees and shrubs that can stand Vermont's long winters, all of which need constant and careful attention. When you're not at the garage working on the cars, you help out in the nursery. You like that work, too.

Right now, though, you are eager to talk to your grandfather about what has happened in the garage. He is working in the farmhouse when you come home.

While you are telling him the story, the phone rings. It's Bill Mazzaro.

"Listen, kid. I've got a plan. It's something I've always wanted to do. I'm going to run my own car! I've saved up the money. We'll have the best stock out there. What do you say, are you with me?" he asks.

Go on to the next page.

You stare at the phone in your hand, not knowing quite what to say.

"Hey, did you hear me? I'm asking you to be my driver! You're good. Together we'll win!"

You almost drop the phone. You were having trouble deciding whether to accept Mike Peterson's offer to be his chief mechanic. And now this! Perhaps you should talk to your grandfather before you just go ahead and make a decision.

Mike Peterson—10

Bill Mazzaro—33

If you make up your mind without talking it over with your grandfather, turn to page 10.

If you'd like to hear what your grandfather thinks before making your decision, turn to page 33.

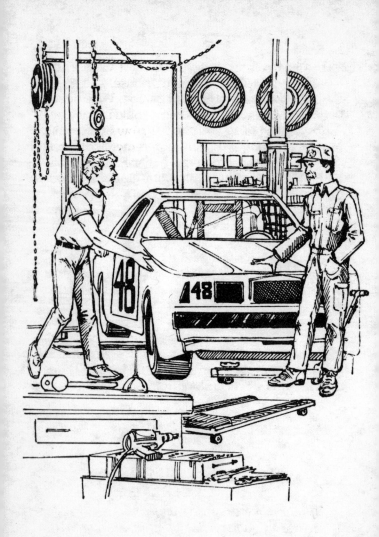

That was painful, but you knew it would be. Now you head for Bill Mazzaro's house. Out back he has a beautifully equipped garage. When you weren't at Mike's or at home you could usually be found at Bill's place. You hesitate now before entering the garage. This is a big moment for you. Then you open the side door and step inside. Bill stands in front of a maroon AMC. It's a 1980 model. It looks like it's in mint condition. It sports the number 48 in bold black letters on a white background.

"Well, what do you think?" Bill says, pointing to the car. "I've been keeping this quiet."

It's a beauty, there's no question about that. You can almost hear the car rounding the big south curve at Thunder Road.

"There's a race Friday at Catamount Park. That's one week from now. How about it, partner? Shall we enter?" Bill walks over to the AMC and pats it affectionately on the right front fender. Then he turns around and gestures for you to examine it yourself.

Turn to page 71.

It's a difficult decision, but you make it on your own. You're barely used to the idea of being offered the position of head mechanic for Mike, and now Bill wants you to *drive*, to actually compete.

"Bill, I'm really flattered, but I can't be your driver. I need some more experience. All the best drivers start out as great mechanics. I still have a lot to learn yet."

"I get it. Peterson spoke to you already, huh? What'd he do, pay you off? You know, I expected a little more loyalty from you after all we've been through together," Bill says bitterly.

Bill's got a point. When Mike was out getting all the attention, you and Bill were working in the background, developing a deep bond. More than once you both worked long into the night, preparing Mike's car for a big race. When you get right down to it, you feel as though you know Bill better than you do Mike.

"Bill, I . . ." you begin to say, but before you can finish, the phone clicks, and you hear a dial tone. Mazzaro has hung up.

"I guess that decides it for me," you say to your grandfather, replacing the phone in its cradle. You head upstairs to study for your algebra exam tomorrow. You try to concentrate, but it's not easy. Finally you decide to get into bed, and before long you are asleep.

Turn to page 27.

After carefully locking the garage door, you rush off to the judges' enclosure. On your way there you pass the garage where Bill Mazzaro is working. It suddenly occurs to you that he'd better know about what happened to the car. He could be in danger, too. Meanwhile you hear Mike's heat announced over the loudspeaker. If you don't withdraw officially before the race begins, he'll start the season off with some penalty points.

If you go directly to the judges' enclosure and withdraw Mike's entry, turn to page 41.

If you decide to warn Bill first, turn to page 26.

Rounding a corner, you barely miss a milk truck. The driver yells at you, his face red and angry. You slow down. There is no sense in getting innocent people hurt.

Rutledge's truck is outside the general store where you first stopped to ask for information about him. Someone climbs into the passenger side. Then Rutledge sees you! He shakes his fist, then pops the clutch. His truck shoots forward and off down the road headed toward Montpelier, the state capital.

Your grandfather's truck is old and not very fast. You hang on as best you can as you follow him.

Turn to page 69.

You know that Mike was mad at Bill. But would he try to burn down his house and garage? It seems impossible to believe.

You see Bill leave. A few seconds later, Mike walks out of his office.

"Oh, hello," he says, uneasily. "I didn't know you were here." He clears his voice nervously. "How's the car?"

"Fine. It could race tonight if you wanted," you reply.

"Good, good. Keep up the good work," he answers distractedly. You watch him leave. Mike is competitive, you think, but he's a good person at heart. He would never try to sabotage Bill. But if Mike didn't try to burn down Bill's garage, then who did?

Your mind comes back to the question again and again over the next few days. By Saturday night's race at Thunder Road, you still have no answer. For the time being you forget all about it as you greet old friends you haven't seen since the end of the season last summer. Word has gotten out about your promotion, and people come up to congratulate you throughout the day. When you pass Bill Mazzaro on the way to lunch, he gives you the cold shoulder. You didn't expect this from him, and you are taken aback.

Turn to page 36.

Weeks later, Bill and Mike are able to patch things up and are working as a team once again. The three of you are at the Catamount Stadium racetrack. It's a twenty-five lap main event, and it's going to be your first race as a driver. You will drive Bill's car, and Mike and Bill are going to be your mechanics.

"Put your helmet on! Tighten that strap!" Bill orders.

"Check your goggles! Stay clear of number 28, he's tough," Mike commands.

"Watch out for the first two curves, that's where the real race begins!"

"And take it easy."

"Remember, you don't have to win your first time out."

"Don't—"

"Watch out—"

"Keep on—"

Turn to page 25.

"I want to go through the safety checklist once again before I let you drive that car," you say, surprised by how serious you sound. Mike looks a bit surprised himself, but he stands aside as you prepare for a final inspection.

You quickly scan the oil and water pressure, look under the car for leaks, listen to the motor run, and examine the suspension bolts. You walk around the car one last time. It's then that you notice something wrong: the right front hubcap isn't on properly. And it wasn't like that earlier.

"Here, Mike, help me with this," you say.

The two of you start to pry off the hubcap with a crowbar when you notice all the lug nuts are missing! The wheel isn't attached to the car!

"Holy cow," Mike yells. "I might have been killed!"

Turn to page 96.

18

The judges leap into action. One man grabs the microphone and announces, "Heat number one, Flying Tigers is canceled. All drivers leave their cars immediately and report to the judge's enclosure. Repeat, leave your cars where they are immediately!"

The crowd is surprised. The drivers are angry. This has never happened before on their track.

The other two judges go off and return with the local sheriff and a state trooper. They turn to you.

"What happened?" the trooper asks.

You explain what happened with the car's wheel. They are upset.

"Are you sure you didn't forget your job and just leave those nuts off?" the official asks.

You are insulted that he could even suggest that. You are tempted to be sarcastic, but you restrain yourself.

As all of you head to the pits to look at Mike's car, Bill Mazzaro comes by and joins you.

"What's up?" he asks. He looks worried.

Turn to page 50.

You glance around the crowd nearby. You see no one who fits the woman's description. Who could it have been?

"Well, she's not here now," you say to the people from the booth. "And I've got to get back to my car. Please let her know that I'm in the garage area and she can find me there if she wants."

You head quickly back to the garage, but as soon as you get there, you feel something's not right. You're not sure what it is, but something feels changed.

"Hey, kid, is the car all ready?" Mike Peterson asks, coming up from behind you. You didn't expect to hear him, so you're a little surprised.

"Uh, yeah, Mike, sure, I mean . . ." you sputter.

"A case of opening night jitters?" he asks, pounding you on the back. "My heat's coming up soon. We better get this machine out to the holding area."

Mike gets into the car and starts the engine.

"Well don't just stand there. Open the door," he asks you impatiently.

You feel panicky. Was it just your imagination that something was wrong, or should you say something to Mike?

If you tell Mike about the incident at the announcer's booth, turn to page 43.

If you decide that you're just nervous, and you let Mike go, turn to page 28.

"We're going to have a nice little talk," Mike says in a tone that is anything but sincere.

But before the talk begins, two black Ford sedans pull into the parking lot, and six people get out. One of them is Bill Mazzaro, and another you recognize as the fire marshal. They head right toward Mike's office.

Rutledge panics and tries to make a run for it, but he is stopped at the doorway by a burly plainclothes policeman.

"I didn't do it. Honest. Mike did it, not me," Rutledge blurts out to the police now gathered around him.

"Shut up," Mike yells.

"We've got some questions to ask the two of you," a man says, flashing his state police identification. "A lot of questions."

The End

To your surprise, sleep comes easily. Eight hours later you are wakened by your grandfather coming into your room.

"Great news, you're in the clear!" he announces.

"What?!" you exclaim, sitting up in bed. Last night seems like a bad dream, and you have trouble figuring out what your grandfather means.

"They've caught the gang who sabotaged Mike's car. Bill played a hunch. He'd been watching this group hanging around the tracks for the last two seasons. They weren't local, and rumor had it they were taking bets on the races."

"So, what happened?" you ask.

"Mazzaro and the state troopers traced them to a motel on the Barre-Montpelier road. It was the woman with the beehive hairdo you saw. She was with two creepy guys in jumpsuits. The minute the woman saw the cops, she confessed! It was as easy as that. And you're in the clear. I know it doesn't bring Mike back, but you've got your whole life ahead of you to make him proud. You'll be the best stock car racer ever."

The End

"He's unconscious," the man replies. "Probably internal injuries. Might even be smoke inhalation."

The shears cut through the metal easily, but they need a power hacksaw to cut through the tubing.

Finally Mike is lifted gently from the car and placed on a backboard. You see the shallow expansion and contraction of his chest and know he is alive.

Once he is firmly strapped to the backboard, one of the medics holds Mike's head while the other carefully removes his goggles. They leave the helmet in place, strapping it to the backboard as well. They take no chances moving him more than they have to because there might well be spinal injuries.

At last they have Mike in the ambulance. You desperately want to go with him, but they won't allow you.

Turn to page 88.

There are so many commands and orders that your head is about to spin. You slip your helmet off. You can barely hear Bill and Mike. You feel secure in your red flame-retardant suit. Your name is over the pocket, and the Allen Lumber logo of your sponsor is sewn on the back. Mike's name and the image of a tractor is sewn on your sleeve.

Your grandfather comes up, grips your hand, and gives you a victory signal as you all exchange the thumbs-up sign.

Turn to page 30.

26

There isn't much time, but if Mike's car is rigged, maybe Bill's car is too. Bill entered the race himself, even though he dislikes driving. You still feel bad about letting him down. You hope he's still not upset with you.

You make it to Bill's just as he is about to pull away.

"Bill, wait. Don't go!" you yell.

He looks up at you. He takes his helmet off and puts it down on the passenger seat.

"What can I do for you?" he asks. His tone isn't very friendly.

"Mike's car has been rigged. The wheel nuts on the front right tire were missing. Check your car. I think somebody's up to something."

Bill stares at you in disbelief. "There's got to be some mistake," he says.

"It's sabotage," you reply.

The two of you head to the officials' booth and withdraw your cars. Other cars are discovered to have similar problems, and the race is canceled. The police take over from here.

Turn to page 15.

Luckily your algebra exam the next day is easier than you expected. By the time the last bell rings, you're in a much better mood. The more you think about it, the more you feel you made the right decision to stay with Mike.

As soon as you get to the garage, you begin work. The first race is only eight days away, but since final exams are coming up, you don't have as much time as you usually have to spend working on the car. Soon you are lost in concentration going through the checklist in preparation for the race. You have just determined there are no water or oil leaks when you hear the loud bang of a door being slammed. Seconds later you hear the sounds of an argument coming from Mike Peterson's office next door.

"So you thought you could stop me with a little arson?" someone shouts. It's the voice of Bill Mazzaro.

"Arson? What are you talking about?" replies Mike Peterson.

"I'm talking about the person who left some dry papers underneath a frayed electrical cord in my garage! If that thing had caught fire, my whole house could have gone up in flames," Bill yells back. "Not to mention my racing car."

Suddenly the door to Mike's office is slammed shut. You hear muffled shouts for a few more minutes. Then it's silent.

Turn to page 14.

"Okay, Mike. Good luck!" you say. You keep telling yourself that all head mechanics get the jitters. "It's only natural," you say to yourself.

Mike edges out onto the track. He is known for the way his cars look. The car is a beauty. Today you feel especially proud of your work.

The crowd roars its approval, but you can barely hear them over the sounds of the engines. You fidget with a broken piece of chain link fence, watching as you wait for the cars to circle the track, jockeying for the starting positions they have been assigned.

The flag drops—and the cars are off!

Turn to page 68.

"Drivers, in your cars," comes the announcement.

You climb into the car over the door that is welded shut. You seat yourself. First your seatbelt and shoulder harness are set. Then the crash cage and roll bars are secured around you. You start the engine. It gives a well-tuned, grumbling roar. Slowly you leave the pit and enter the track.

Your hands tremble a bit at first, but you calm down. Your car is with the others, in the position you have been assigned.

The flag drops!

AND YOU'RE OFF!

Your blood pulses with a fantastic rush. You see things clearer and better than you ever have in your whole life. Twenty-five laps go by in what seems like seconds.

Finally, the checkered flag!

You finish in ninth place. You didn't win, but it's not bad for your first time out.

The End

Later, Mike and Bill patch up their friendship and agree to work together as a team, running not one but two cars—one of them driven by you!

A week later the police announce in an article in the local paper that they are onto a ring of gamblers who have been fixing races throughout the New England area. Races at Thunder Road will start back up in three days.

The End

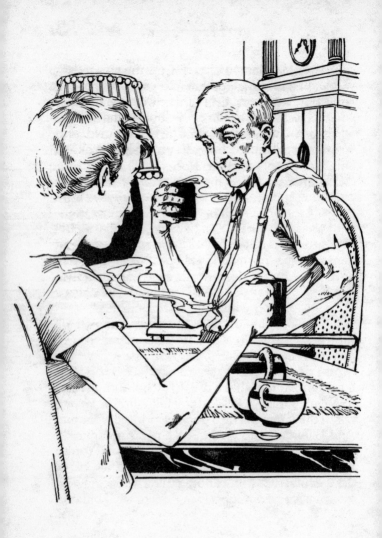

You tell Bill Mazzaro you need some time to talk with your grandfather before you make a decision. After you hang up the phone, your grandfather smiles. He sits you down at the table in the kitchen and pours cider from a jug. The cider is cold, and you can smell the fresh apples you helped pick last fall.

The two of you talk for some time about the problems and the opportunities presented by Bill's and Mike's offers. When your grandfather says, "Follow your heart," your heart says to go with Bill Mazzaro as his driver. So it's decided, but you wait until the next morning to tell both Bill and Mike of your decision. "Life is never easy," your grandfather tells you as you go off to school. "It's always difficult deciding what is best for yourself."

It is difficult. Mike seems stunned when you tell him your decision. "What? You mean you're going to drive for Bill? I can't believe it."

You do your best to make him feel better. You even remind him that it was Bill who brought you to Mike's garage. "Mike, don't take this the wrong way. I think this will be a good opportunity for me. And Bill's going to give me a chance to drive!"

"Yeah, and you'll probably kill yourself. You're not ready yet. A year, maybe two, and then okay, drive. But now, I don't know. I think it's wrong. But it's your life, kid. Good luck," Mike says bitterly.

Turn to page 9.

"Mike! Mike!" you scream as you leap over the fence. The ambulance crew is just arriving, lights flashing, as you hit the track and head for the tangle of broken cars.

"Hey kid, where are you going?" someone yells. You ignore the question as you thread your way through the pileup. A fire truck pulls up, the firemen leaping off and grabbing their hoses as they try to put out the fires.

Finally you work your way over to Mike's car. The side and front are squashed in. The impact was so severe that the heavy metal tubing surrounding him is grotesquely twisted. Mike is slumped forward, the shoulder harness barely supporting him.

Your heart is beating rapidly. You can't believe what you see.

"Easy. There's nothing you can do," a man says, putting his hand on your shoulder to steady you.

Two firemen from the rescue squad move toward Mike's car with metal shears. Quickly they work them into place and begin to cut the metal frame of the car so they can get Mike out.

"Is he dead?" you ask.

Turn to page 23.

At dusk, people begin to enter the race grounds. The first qualifying heat is about to begin when an announcement comes over the PA system:

"Will Mike Peterson's mechanic come to the announcer's booth immediately. There is a family emergency. Repeat, will Mike Peterson's mechanic come to the announcer's booth immediately?"

A family emergency? What kind of family emergency? Your grandfather stopped by only minutes ago to say hello before getting a seat in the bleachers. And both of your parents live out of state. You take a quick look around the empty garage. It'll be okay to leave the car for a few minutes, you think as you take off.

Turn to page 49.

"Hey, wait a minute!" you shout, tugging at the woman's arm. "You can't leave! I'm going to call the police!"

The heavyset man swings his arm in a swift arc and brutally smacks you on the head with a heavy wrench.

As you sink to the ground, the last sight you have is that of the three of them laughing as they walk away. Then you black out.

When you come to, you slowly make your way over to the pits. It is then that you learn that Mike has died.

The End

You think it would be best to pull out of the race.

Bill understands. "There will be plenty of opportunities this summer. Now, let's go to the doctor and get that arm of yours checked out."

The injury to your shoulder is just as you thought—you have some slight tissue damage. But it takes a lot longer to heal than you expected. You're unable to race at all this summer, and when the fall comes, you spend all of your time in the library, studying for your college classes.

The End

You turn from the wreckage on the track knowing that at best you would be in the way. Pushing against the crowd, you try and get to the officials' booth.

The crowd at Thunder Road is on its feet, people craning to see, pushing and shoving to get nearer to the wreckage.

Who would do this to Mike? you ask yourself. Who would want to really hurt him? You run through in your mind the names and faces of possible suspects: competitors that Mike has beaten for the trophy in past races; farmers with financial problems that led to Mike's taking equipment—or even whole farms—as payment. And then there's Bill Mazzaro.

When you think about it, Mike could have many enemies. You don't know where to begin. But before you speculate, you must speak with the police. When you saw the wheel spin off, you knew that the car had been sabotaged. You tightened those lug nuts yourself, twice to be sure. You checked the axles, the rims, the wheels. There were no signs of wear or tear, no indication that anything was wrong.

The ACT officials are not in their booth. There is a policeman standing outside the booth. He is talking into the radio. You stop dead in your tracks. You know he's talking about Mike when you hear him say, "Maybe he won't make it."

Turn to page 51.

You don't have much time: you run to the judges' area.

"Hey, someone, anyone, I need to withdraw!" you shout at the judges who sit behind a table.

"Not now, kid, we're busy," one of them says.

"Final race for heat one of Flying Tigers. Repeat, this is the final call, heat one," the judge announces over the PA.

"You've got to listen," you demand. "I'm Mike Peterson's head mechanic. Here are my credentials." You are insistent. "We are withdrawing from the race. Someone has been tampering with our car."

That gets their attention. The ACT officials are really strict about safety precautions. They are always kicking people out of races if they don't have proper fire-retardant suits, or if the roll bars and crash cage aren't welded the right way, or for any one of a number of reasons. You used to think their attention to detail was a little excessive, but you appreciate their concern now.

"What did you say?" the judge asks, surprised.

"Our car has been sabotaged. We're withdrawing," you reply.

Turn to page 18.

It's really late now. Finally they say you can go.

"Think it over," the detective says. "We're not charging you, but you're our most likely suspect."

You walk out of the room and into the front office feeling as though your entire world has suddenly collapsed all around you. It all seems so crazy. Mike's dead, and you're a suspect. What should have been a great summer has turned into a nightmare.

Turn to page 52.

"Something very odd just happened, Mike. Did you hear them page me to the announcer's booth?" you ask him.

He shakes his head no.

"Well, an announcement came over the PA system that there was a family emergency for Mike Peterson's mechanic," you begin. "But when I got there a few minutes later, the woman, who said she was my Aunt Ida, had disappeared."

"It was probably meant for Bill. Not everyone knows about his leaving yet," Mike replies. "Did they say what kind of emergency?"

"Something about my cousin Jimmy having broken his arm. But I don't have a cousin Jimmy," you tell Mike. "Or an Aunt Ida."

"It's nothing, kid—just a mistake. Don't worry about it. Now if I don't get into the holding area for the upcoming heat, I'm going to be disqualified."

If you let Mike drive off, turn to page 28.

If you exercise your right as head mechanic to hold up the car for inspection, turn to page 17.

"Well if you don't believe me," you plead, "ask the announcer. He'll tell you about the lady with the beehive hairdo."

But it's no use. The way they see it you were either incompetent and failed to check the wheel lugs or, even worse, you were paid to leave those lug nuts off by someone who wanted Mike dead or out of the running.

For now you are stripped of your racing license and warned by the police, both state and local, that you are a suspect of sabotage.

When you finally get home that night, your grandfather sits you down. With kindness he tells you, "Hang in there. Truth is on your side, and it will win out in the end, even if it doesn't seem so right now."

You only wish you could share his optimism.

The End

It turns out that you are not really hurt. And your shoulder is not in bad shape either. Three weeks later you are back behind the wheel, racing in Catamount Park.

Your next race is a tough one, with experienced drivers, including several known for their daring.

But luck comes your way. A jam-up on the eighth lap knocks out six cars! You slide by, and when they start the race again, you are in third place and moving up.

Soon you are in second place.

Then, unbelievably, you move into the lead. You hit the finish line—and the checkered flag is yours!

The End

For now you stay where you are and watch the races. There are two bad crashes, but miraculously, no one is injured. It's a fairly good night at Thunder Road. Several of the drivers are really crazy. You try to learn as much as you can from watching every race and every move.

School and your old job working for Mike are behind you, and the summer lies ahead. Your first race is coming up, and the checkered flag will soon come down.

The End

"I'll see what I can do," you say to Mike.

When you talk to Bill, his reaction is just what you thought it would be.

"Are you joking? No way."

"Well, just talk to him. He needs you now," you say.

Finally Bill agrees to at least go over to the pits.

The next ten minutes are like watching a TV sitcom, you think. Watching two grown men act like children is both sad and amusing. Finally Mike and Bill shake hands. You knew they would, or at least you hoped they would. The only lingering doubt you have is why Mike ever hired someone with Rutledge's reputation. It's a side of Mike's character that you have never seen before. You remind yourself to be careful and watch and listen for anything out of the ordinary.

Turn to page 54.

"Hello, I'm Mike Peterson's mechanic," you say to the woman in the PA booth. "I was just paged."

"Right, your Aunt Ida stopped by. She needed a ride to the hospital—your little cousin Jimmy fell from the bleachers, and he broke his arm."

"Aunt Ida? I don't have an Aunt Ida. Or a cousin Jimmy. Are you sure it was me she wanted?" you ask.

"Just a second. I didn't take the message. I'll go find out who did," she replies.

The woman returns a few minutes later with a man who tells you, "It was a tall lady with a beehive hairdo. She asked for Mike Peterson's mechanic. I'm positive. In fact, I thought it was a little funny that she didn't use your name, but she seemed pretty upset. She said she'd wait right here."

Turn to page 19.

When you tell Bill what happened to the wheel of the car, he is shocked. He is an honest and dedicated driver. The thought of this kind of crime in his sport infuriates him.

"I'd like to get my hands on those crooks," he snaps.

Then he turns to the officials. "This here is one of the best mechanics I've seen. Might be young, but one of the best." He means you, and you are proud to hear his praise.

First the officials look at Mike's car. Then they examine all the other cars on the track. Two other cars are similarly rigged.

"That's enough. We're closing the track tonight pending an investigation," the head ACT official says.

Turn to page 31.

"Excuse me, sir, but I need to talk with you a moment," you ask the policeman.

"I'm sorry, kid, but I'm busy. We've got some real problems here tonight." The officer turns back to his radio. "We can't even find the head mechanic," he says into the receiver. "They say he split right after the crash. Sounds suspicious to me."

"Hey, I'm the head mechanic!" you say.

"I told you, we're very busy here. I have no time for games," he replies.

"But I am! Look. See, here's the pass." You hold out the official pass that gives you entrance to the track and the pits. It has your name, picture, and identifies you as head mechanic; Mike Peterson, driver.

The policeman takes a closer look.

Turn to page 61.

"Hang in there," comes the familiar voice of your grandfather. Standing next to him is Bill Mazzaro. "We got here as soon as we could. We've been doing a little snooping. That is, Bill here has."

You have never been so glad to see anyone in your whole life. You throw your arms around Bill, the death of your friend Mike hitting you for the first time. "Come, let's go," Bill says.

The police say something, but you don't even hear it. Your mind is so confused that all you can do is follow Bill and your grandfather out the door and over to Bill's car.

"We'll get to the bottom of this tomorrow. You try and get some rest," your grandfather says.

Turn to page 22.

For the time being you are at the races, and Bill is once again Mike's mechanic. This year you will have your chance to drive, too. Things are very exciting.

"Drivers, in your cars," comes the announcement over the loudspeaker.

And the race is on.

The End

The fire marshal is interested in what you said, and he calls the police lieutenant over to talk with you. Pretty soon they are talking at you so loud you can't think straight. You wish you could walk away and go back home to your grandfather. You think that maybe you should have just kept quiet.

Suddenly a policeman breaks in with a comment that stops everyone for a moment. "My men checked on Peterson's whereabouts. He was three hundred miles away at a tractor auction in northern New Jersey. He's in the clear."

A wave of relief comes over you. Mike is innocent, and you are no longer the focus of their questioning.

"Thanks for your help. But don't worry, we'll get to the bottom of this yet."

You walk home slowly. Your grandfather will know what to do. Your career as a race driver is over—for now.

What a way to begin the summer.

The End

You decide to confront the woman now, before you lose sight of her.

You slip through the crowd as fast as you can, but it's difficult. People are excited by the accident, and many are pressing up against the fence to get a better view. The woman with the beehive hairdo still stands by the booth.

Finally you make your way over to her.

"Excuse me, but . . ." you begin.

"Whaddya want, kid? I'm busy," the woman replies in a harsh voice.

"Are you the one who left a message and had me paged?"

"Just what are you getting at?"

At that moment two men dressed in fancy jumpsuits, the kind used by the drivers, come up to the woman.

"Let's go, Gladys. We're done here. Good job," the larger one of the two men says.

"Beat it," Gladys says to you, laughing. "I've got places to go, things to do, and money to spend."

Turn to page 37.

"Come on, Bill. There's a lot of work to do, but I think I can juggle it all. Let's go for it," you say.

"Great, kid. You've got heart," Mazzaro says. "We can get this car all ready and start your training in no time."

"Let's get at it," you reply.

In between working on the car and training to drive, you try to study for your exams. Your grandfather is worried that you are spreading yourself too thin, but you assure him that you are handling everything. It's tough, but it's only for a short period of time. You study late at night, and when you are taking your exams, you call on every ounce of skill and energy that you have.

In the fall you will be going to business college. You've already been accepted, and you have done very well in the past, so you are not overly worried. But you can't flunk. Your grades must be passing if you are to get financial aid. And you also need that scholarship money.

Go on to the next page.

After school you work on the car. You also get in some driving practice in the field behind your grandfather's farm.

Your grandfather takes care of details like getting a special fire-retardant suit, a helmet, goggles, and gloves. He has become very supportive.

As the day of the race gets closer, you find it difficult to think of anything else. Finally exams are behind you, and the future looks good, at least as far as college is concerned.

Turn to page 98.

"Hey! You're for real. Hold on," he shouts into the radio set. "I've got the mechanic. He's standing right here!"

There is an ominous tone in his voice.

The policeman grabs you roughly by the arm, but you manage to squirm free.

"Don't give me any trouble. We're going to the station. You've got some explaining to do."

This is not what you expected. The officer suspects *you!* You want an explanation, too. But you wonder if it would be best for you to go with the officer and find out.

*If you run away into the crowd,
turn to page 79.*

*If you go with the officer quietly,
turn to page 65.*

"Listen, you could be in a lot of trouble. I mean big time," the chief official says.

The state trooper steps in with the standard, "Anything you say can and will be used against you . . ."

"Look," you begin, "I can explain everything." You talk fast and hard. The faces peering at you aren't overly sympathetic. This accident is serious, and they are eager to fix the blame on someone.

Turn to page 44.

Somehow you manage to get your grandfather's truck out of the ditch and back onto the road. The left fender is damaged, but you can drive.

Your instinct says to chase Rutledge, but you realize at this point it's best to go for the police. You check out your arm and leg. You seem to be all right aside from some minor soreness.

There isn't much time to waste.

"How did he know who I was?" you ask out loud. Maybe somebody at the corner store tipped him off.

You accelerate and roar off down the road.

Turn to page 12.

"I need more time to practice," you tell Bill. "I think I'll be more prepared by the end of the summer."

"I understand," he says. "We'll work on the car and your driving, but at a slower pace. This way you can study, and when you're done, we can have fun. We'll still go to the races. But just as spectators."

Bill is fun to be with, and the two of you get a lot done over the following weeks. Your exams go well, and your driving practice is going well, too.

One Saturday night, you and Bill make it to the speedway at Thunder Road, and there you see Mike Peterson. He has a new mechanic, a guy named Rutledge who has a reputation for being dishonest. Bill caught him last year with illegal weighting equipment in his Ford.

It would be nice to say hello to Mike, but you're not sure how he'll react. It might be best to just say nothing.

If you go up to speak with Mike, turn to page 82.

If you leave things as they are, turn to page 87.

"But I didn't do anything," you say.

"Well, all I know is there are some serious questions that need to be answered. And I'm taking you in."

He leads you to the cruiser, and you slide into the backseat. It's an old Chevy 4 X 4. This officer is a local sheriff paid by the town to patrol the racetrack. He has the power and authority to arrest you, but you wonder whether or not he isn't exceeding those powers right now.

"Where are we going?" you demand.

"State police barracks," he replies coldly. Then the car leaps forward, roaring out of the driveway with its lights flashing. The trip to the barracks takes about fifteen minutes. The whole way there you worry about Mike more than yourself. You are confident that you can explain everything, but you are desperate to find out how Mike is doing. Then the radio signals several times, and the officer picks up the mike.

"Unit 3 here. What's the status on Peterson?" he asks.

Turn to page 67.

There is a pause, and then you hear the words, "I'm afraid he didn't make it."

Both you and the policeman are silent. The finality of the words hits you slowly. You can't believe it. You remain quiet, thinking about Mike. Slowly you start to cry.

"Like I said," the officer starts to say, "you're wanted for questioning. Somebody tipped us off that you were paid to rig Mike Peterson's car. Paid big money!"

"But that's crazy!" you yell. "Mike was my friend!"

"Save that for the funeral," he says.

At last the car slips into the parking lot at the state police barracks. You are frightened. What if they don't believe your story? you think as you reluctantly get out of the car.

Turn to page 112.

Mike is in the number two spot. His car shoots forward, the engine roaring as the tires spin down the straightaway. Three cars are right on his tail.

As they enter the turn, the right front wheel on Mike's car spins off, careening up the banked turn! It flies into the air before dropping out of sight behind some bushes.

Two cars blast right into Mike as he spins around, coming to rest in the middle of the track facing the oncoming cars.

One after the other, cars pile up. Other cars roar off onto the grass, avoiding collision.

Suddenly a gas tank bursts into flames. There is so much smoke and confusion that you can't tell what's really happening. You know Mike is in trouble, and you want to help him, but you're not sure what to do.

If you leap the fence and rush to get Mike out of his car, turn to page 34.

If you run for the police, turn to page 39.

There is traffic on the road, and Rutledge is unable to pass. He is caught behind a tractor trailer chugging up a long hill with a steep grade. You are on his bumper, giving him little room to get away.

In sheer frustration, Rutledge pulls out in the left lane and tries to pass the truck. It is a bad move, and it is his last!

The accident takes the lives of four people: Rutledge, his passenger, and the two people in the car coming the other way. You feel guilty for having forced him into making the dangerous move. "I should have called the police," you say to the witnesses. "Then this wouldn't have happened."

Although you know Rutledge wasn't a good person, you have his death and the deaths of the other innocent people on your conscience. The memory stays with you, and you relive it every time you get in a car. Out of respect, you give up stock car racing.

The End

You realize that before you ask Mike for his help you need to do some more investigating. Mike has always taught you to be totally prepared for whatever you do, whether working on an engine, taking a test in school, or even playing soccer.

"Preparation and discipline: they're the foundation of success," he would say to you. And from everything you have seen, it certainly works. Mike is successful in business and in racing.

But Bill Mazzaro says that Mike is too tough on everybody, including himself. Bill thinks that you've got to ease off a bit here and there, follow intuition sometimes, be more spontaneous. Bill says he can "feel" what's wrong with an engine. He doesn't need the plans to get an engine working. And Bill is a good mechanic, really good.

So you try to do both: prepare for the investigation *and* follow your intuition. When you get up the next morning, the first thing you do is head for the library to look up any information on fires, arson, and insurance investigations. You also plan to read up on the law about arson, evidence, suspects, etc.

Turn to page 102.

"Bill, I'm not ready," you say, surprising yourself with your sudden doubt.

Bill looks disappointed. Even though he is more than twenty years older than you, his judgment is not always very good. Some people have said that his enthusiasm gets in the way of his reasoning.

"But the car is almost ready. Don't you think—"

You hold up your hand, stopping him right there. Driving a racing car is a matter of life and death. You have a license to race. As a matter of fact, you just got it this spring, two days after your birthday. But you never imagined that you would be using it so soon.

"Let me think it over, Bill. I just want to be sure I'm ready. I'll give you an answer tomorrow."

"Okay, but we should get to work now so we don't lose any time if you do decide to race at Catamount Park. That race is coming up fast," Bill says.

Turn to page 107.

Suddenly a black 1976 Chevy Nova comes screeching down the narrow dirt road at a speed well in excess of sixty miles per hour. You do your best to avoid the head-on collision, but as you pull to the right, Rutledge, behind the wheel of the Chevy, swerves and fishtails into your pickup. *Rutledge!*

The noise of smashing glass and the tearing of metal sounds horrible. You slam on the brakes, swerving off the road and ending up in a ditch. The Chevy continues down the road, accelerating. Rutledge does not even try to stop and see if you are hurt.

Your right shoulder throbs, and you feel pain in your left leg as well. Dizziness and nausea begin to overwhelm you.

Turn to page 63.

74

The day of the race arrives, and you decide to go through with it.

Pain races through your shoulder as you climb into the car. You have trouble putting on the shoulder harness, but finally you are set, the engine running, your heart beating a mile a minute, as you wait for the race to begin.

You are in the third heat, way back in the lineup. It's nighttime. The lights are on, and the crowd is anxious for the race to begin.

The flag drops. You're off!

Quickly you tear down the straightaway, sliding through the first corner, up the bank, and down on the straights.

Suddenly a car smashes into you from behind, but you go on.

Then another slam, and you fall back. You round the curve, go up the bank—and then off the track, into the bushes.

The ambulance screeches out to you, the red light flashing. The race is stopped.

"How are you feeling?" a man with an EMS badge asks.

"Great, just great," you reply, glad to be out of the race—at least for the time being.

Turn to page 45.

Finally the two of you draw up a chart:

TASKS Brakes	Saturday	Sunday	Monday	Tuesday *	Wednesday	Thursday	Friday *
Roll bars	*	*					
Cage	*	*					
Gas tanks			*				
Fuel lines			*				
Tires & wheels				*			*
Engine tuning						*	*
Body paint						*	
Glass removal						*	
Suspension	*	*	*				
Exhaust		*		*			
Entry fees					*		
Application					*		
Uniform					*		

You place a star on the chart in the column for work scheduled. As you complete your work, you will check it off.

Go on to the next page.

You attach the chart to the wall and stand back, surveying your work.

"There's a lot to do, Bill. And not a lot of time, either."

"There sure is," he says, eyeing the impressive chart. Right above it are two old black and yellow flags, victory symbols Bill has picked up years back. "Hey, we forgot something," he says.

"What?" you ask, sure that you haven't forgotten anything.

"Training. Driver training. As you said, preparing the car is one thing; being prepared to drive is another."

"You're right," you reply. How in the world will you manage to get everything in? you wonder. Working on the car, driver training, studying for exams—there's a lot to do. You are really worried. Things are coming on too fast, there's too much. Before you go any further, you have to make your decision.

If you put off racing until after your exams are over, turn to page 80.

If you try to juggle everything in one week, turn to page 58.

If you postpone racing until the end of the summer, turn to page 64.

"You can't accuse someone just on a hunch," your grandfather says. "If the man you suspect did do it, he could be dangerous. Stay out of sight and watch. Listen, maybe even make a couple of phone calls. But don't under any circumstances try to find that fellow. That's police work."

"Thanks," you reply, but you have already decided to go against what your grandfather says, just this once. First you'd like to get Mike Peterson in on it. You think he'll help, particularly if you can gather some hard evidence. A little digging around would be a good idea.

If you go directly to Mike and ask for his help, turn to page 95.

If you do some more investigating first, turn to page 70.

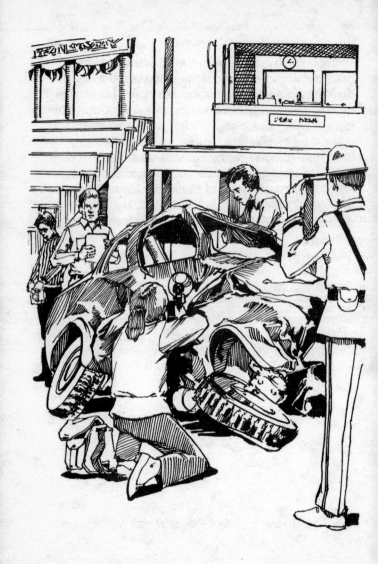

I've got to get out of here! you say to yourself. With great determination you slip away from the policeman and join the crowd of people milling around in front of the stands. Working your way through the crowd, you plan to get to the ACT officials and talk with them.

"Stop!" you hear the officer shout, but his voice is lost in the blare of noise from the loudspeakers.

You make it to the track, and there you see three of the ACT officials plus two of the track's top brass. They are standing next to Mike's car looking at the front end. A photographer is busy taking a series of shots, getting different angles and distances. A state trooper joins the group. He is tall and strongly built, and he is not smiling.

You march right up to the group. "Gentlemen, I'm Mike Peterson's head mechanic."

"We've been looking for you," the chief official says. Then he pauses. "But you're just a kid."

"I'm old enough," you reply.

Turn to page 62.

You'll have plenty of time to race after you take your exams, you decide.

That week, while you are studying, you hear fire engines. From your bedroom window you see the orange glow of fire. It seems to be coming from Bill's house. By the time you get there, his garage is a smoking ruin. There is nothing left but the hulk of metal that used to be the maroon AMC and assorted hunks of steel that were tools.

The police and fire marshal question you at length about the fire.

"Do you think Peterson did it? Or did Mazzaro do it himself?"

"Hey, what are you getting at?" you reply. "It just happened. Fires happen, you know."

The fire marshal winks at the police officer.

"Well, maybe you're right. But maybe, just maybe, this fire was set. Revenge? Insurance money? Who knows?"

Then you remember that remark Mike Peterson made the other day—about how things got too hot for Bill Mazzaro. And how they just might get *hotter.*

At the time you thought he was referring to the pressure of racing. But now you're not so sure.

Go on to the next page.

This is one of the toughest decisions of your life, you feel. Mike Peterson has been your friend and mentor for years. You'd feel like a traitor turning in one of your best friends. On the other hand, Bill's shop is destroyed. As you kick idly through the charred wood of the building, uncovering blackened, useless tools, you become angry. Bill Mazzaro is too careful to make a foolish mistake and leave oily rags around or overload an electrical circuit. And he cared too much about his car to destroy it on purpose.

If you tell the police and fire marshal about Mike's comment, turn to page 100.

If you investigate the cause of the fire on your own, turn to page 91.

82

"I'm going to say hello to Mike. Coming with me?" you ask Bill.

"I've nothing to say to him. Why waste your time?"

"I've got nothing to lose," you say, trying to sound optimistic.

You use your pass to get to the pits. Mike is standing by his car. He doesn't look too happy.

"What's up, Mike?" you ask.

"Oh, I just had to fire my new mechanic. He wasn't very good, and I couldn't trust him. I guess I'm going to have to drop out of the race."

"Hey, how about Bill and me? We can be your crew and help you out. I can ask him," you say.

"He'd never agree," Mike says.

"It doesn't hurt to ask. You two were friends, you know."

"Well, you're wasting your breath. On him, I mean, not me. I sure could use you two. We could make a team again, even run two cars, Bill's and mine." Mike pauses. "But he'd never agree. It's bad blood now."

Turn to page 47.

While in the library you look up articles on last year's races in the local newspaper. There on the sports page, down at the bottom of the July third paper, the day after the race, you see an article describing the illegal weighting of a racing car. It gives the driver's name: Tom Rutledge of Winooski, Vermont.

With that information, you look up his name in the telephone book. It's listed all right. You dial the number.

It rings six times. Your heart beats faster with each ring.

"Hello? Whaddayawant?"

It's a woman's voice.

"Uh . . . uh . . ."

"Speak up. I can't hear you," the woman says.

"Tom Rutledge. Does he live there?" It's a foolish question, you realize, but it's too late.

"No, he moved to Calais about two months ago. And good riddance!" She hangs up, and you breathe a sigh of reflief.

Go on to the next page.

Calais is a small town. It should be easy to find Tom Rutledge there, or at least check up on him. You can use your grandfather's truck. Then you remember what your grandfather said: the man could be dangerous. Maybe it would be best to tell Mike what you have been up to and ask him to come with you.

*If you go to Calais on your own,
turn to page 104.*

*If you ask Mike to go with you,
turn to page 101.*

You realize it would be best to leave things as they are between you and Mike. You have the whole summer to settle your differences.

"Let's watch the race," you say to Bill.

The stands are crowded, but you finally find a seat. There are a lot of announcements. One of them surprises you. It says, "Car 38, Mike Peterson, is withdrawing from tonight's races."

"What's that all about, Bill?" you ask.

"Don't know, don't care," he replies. "Probably mechanical problems. Mike never has been good with machines."

Turn to page 46.

Bill Mazzaro emerges from the crowd of people now working to disentangle the wreckage.

"You okay?" he asks.

"Bill, I think Mike's going to die," you reply. "He's hurt badly."

"Easy. He's tough. He'll pull through. You'll see."

"Bill, I think somebody sabotaged his car. I know they did."

Bill is leading you away from the track up to the hillside where the picnic tables are. You follow him automatically, still deeply shocked by all you have seen.

"Did you hear what I said, Bill? I think someone sabotaged Mike's car."

"I heard you. That's a serious charge. What makes you think it was sabotage? Wheels come off. Not when I put them on, but they do. It happens a lot."

You tell Bill about the PA announcement and the phony message you were given.

"We've got to look at the car," you say.

"The officials will do that," Bill replies.

"Well, I'm going down there. I'm Mike's mechanic. I have to go. Are you coming?" you ask Bill.

"Sorry, kid, but I've got other things to do."

Turn to page 93.

"Hey there. I'm the new head mechanic here," the man says, introducing himself.

Your heart drops. You can't believe you've found him.

"Uh, what's going on? What are you doing?" you manage to ask.

"Not much. A few changes here and there. We're going to win with this beauty."

You just know that he's up to his old tricks, and you fear that Mike is in on it.

Turn to page 113.

You have always been interested in detective work. Solving problems, making up theories, has always fascinated you. It's probably what makes you a good mechanic. Maybe you can investigate the cause of this fire on your own.

You begin with Bill Mazzaro. You walk over to his home and go inside. You are so much a part of his family that you don't have to knock.

"Bill, this is terrible. What do you think happened?"

"I don't know. I just don't know. My whole savings went up in that fire. All my money was in that shop. I've lost everything."

Bill's wife Betsy comforts him. You know how hard he has worked and what the garage meant to him. It was his plan for the future to be on his own, independent of Mike Peterson. Now those plans are all over.

Bill is of no help at this time; he can't even begin to think clearly about who might have done this to him. "I have no enemies," he says. "Even Mike Peterson would never do anything like this to me."

Turn to page 109.

Mike gets out of his chair and walks over to you. You notice that his face has turned whiter, and he has become very serious. "What did you find?"

The way he asks the question, and his tone and intensity, scare you. You back up to the office door.

"Nothing, really. I mean nothing that anyone would be interested in."

"I'll decide that," Mike replies. "Now talk." He hits the button on the intercom to his garage workshop.

"Get in here quick," Mike snaps into the speaker.

Moments later, Tom Rutledge walks into the room, wiping his grease-stained hands with a rag.

"What's up, boss?" Rutledge asks.

"Ask the kid."

You freeze. This is like a nightmare with no hope of waking up.

"I don't know anything, I promise. I just thought we could help Mazzaro. He's in trouble, that's all." You wish you could get out of the office, but Rutledge is between you and the door.

Turn to page 20.

You head back down to the track. Pausing for a second, you watch Bill as he blends into the crowd by the grandstands. That's when you spot a woman with a beehive hairdo who fits the description the announcers gave of the woman who had you paged.

The woman stands next to one of the concession booths where they sell hot dogs. She seems to be scanning the crowd, looking for someone. You're not sure what to do. This is your chance to find out the answers to some of your questions, and you don't want to lose sight of the woman. On the other hand, it might be more helpful to tell the police what you suspect and have them handle it.

If you confront the woman, turn to page 56.

If you report the woman to the police, turn to page 51.

Before you go any further with your investigation, you think it best to visit with Mike and ask for his help.

Mike is in the tractor showroom talking to a customer when you pull up on your mountain bike. He sees you and waves.

"Be with you in a minute," he says.

"I'll meet you in the shop," you reply.

The shop is one of your favorite places, and it feels good to be back there. To your surprise, there is someone in there working on Mike's latest racer. You recognize the man at once as the one who rigged his racing car and had his license revoked—he's the man you are looking for!

Turn to page 89.

You and Mike stare at the tire, your mouths hanging open. Mike would probably have made it around the track a few times, long enough to get up to speed. Then, as he was taking a tight corner, the force would have knocked the tire right off.

"I've had just about enough of this. Mazzaro has gone too far this time. I'm calling the police," Mike says, seething.

"Mazzaro?" you say. "Why would Bill do a thing like this?"

"He probably thinks I tried to burn his shop," Mike answers.

"Well, did you?" you ask, finally glad to get your question out in the open.

"Of course not. If I want to get even with Bill, I'll beat him on the racetrack fair and square," Mike replies.

"Then my guess is that the woman with the beehive hairdo is after the two of you. It's possible that whoever she is or whoever she's working for didn't know that you and Bill had split. You've been a pretty formidable team for the past several seasons. Lots of drivers or sponsors might want the two of you out of the running this year," you state.

"Yeah, but how would we ever figure out who?" Mike asks.

Go on to the next page.

"I say we start by finding 'Aunt Ida,' " you reply. "She's obviously the lead."

"You're right. You go to the judges' enclosure and withdraw our entry. I'll go to the PA booth and try to get a better description of what she looked like. With that hairdo, she shouldn't be too hard to find."

"Right, I'll meet you there," you nod.

Turn to page 11.

The next day something totally unexpected happens.

While riding your dirt bike back home from Bill's garage, you slam into a rock. The bike flips back on you, and in the fall you partially dislocate your shoulder.

The pain is intense for a moment, and then, as you move your arm, the shoulder settles back into its socket. Cradling your arm with the other, you look in dismay at your broken dirt bike. It could have been worse, you console yourself.

You decide not to tell your grandfather or Bill. You'd rather not go to the doctor.

By morning your arm is really sore. You can move it, but it throbs. Reading up in a book on accidents and injuries that your grandfather keeps in the library, you find that soft tissue damage, which is probably what you have, takes a long time to heal.

The race is tomorrow.

If you pull out of the race, turn to page 38.

If you decide to go through with it, turn to page 74.

Approaching the fire marshal, the man responsible for investigating and determining the cause of all fires in his district, you feel justified in telling him what Mike said, but you hesitate. You don't feel right about getting Mike in trouble.

"What is it?" he asks you. This man has probably heard it all, you think. His eyes watch you, but he smiles as if to dispel your fear and encourage you to speak up. "What's on your mind?"

Turn to page 110.

You head for Mike's office. "Mike, I need your help," you say as you walk in. He smiles and motions for you to sit down.

"I was hoping you'd come back," Mike says. "Bill's not the man for you. Look what has happened already. He's through."

"That's what I'm here about, Mike. I think we should help him." You wait for Mike's response. You notice what might be anger in Mike's face, but you could be wrong.

"Okay, tell me how. But I can't hire him back. I've already got a new mechanic."

"Mike, I think someone torched his shop. I think the fire was set on purpose."

Mike shakes his head and says, "That's serious. Can you prove it?"

"I think so. I've been doing some investigating. I need your help."

"I don't know. I think you're on the wrong track. It was just an electrical fire. Bill was careless. I think you should leave it alone."

"But Mike, there were burn spots in the garage, like someone put gasoline on the sides of the building and then lit it," you tell him. With this information you notice him perk up.

"Are you sure? Cops tell you about that?" Mike asks.

"Yes. And besides that, I found something else on my own," you reply.

Turn to page 92.

It is a huge task, and after talking with the reference librarian, you decide to narrow the field to laws about arson and evidence of criminal intent. You also choose to look up case studies of typical "set" fires and any articles that describe the type of person who becomes an arsonist.

Again, the field of information is huge. But using the computer to search the subject, you narrow it down a bit. Three hours pass in the library, three hours you could have used studying for exams, but you get fascinated by the law, by the information on fires, and by the psychological profiles of arsonists.

Turn to page 108.

You use your grandfather's truck and head for Calais on your own.

It's a small town. It's got one general store with a single gas pump outside, a post office, and a town hall. There's a nice pond, not big enough to be called a lake, and a number of dairy farms.

You inquire in the store.

"Anybody know Tom Rutledge?" you ask a couple behind the counter.

"Unfortunately, yes," the man says. "And if I were you, I wouldn't want to know him."

That's quite a statement to start a conversation with, you think.

"What'd he do?" you persist.

"It's what he doesn't do, like pay bills. His credit is no good here," the man says. "And it only took him a few months to establish that. He's been hanging around here on and off since March. Finally moved up full-time in April. He's no good, that's my opinion."

"You know, Dick, you shouldn't speak so. This person might be family," the woman standing next to the man says.

"Don't worry, ma'am, I don't think much of him either," you say. "Do you know where he lives or what he does?"

Go on to the next page.

She gives you a closer look.

"My advice is stay away from him. He's trouble." But she tells you where he lives. It's about six miles out of town on top of a hill.

Driving out to check out his house, you wonder what you will do if you run into him. "Well, I'll worry about that when the time comes," you say to yourself out loud.

Turn to page 72.

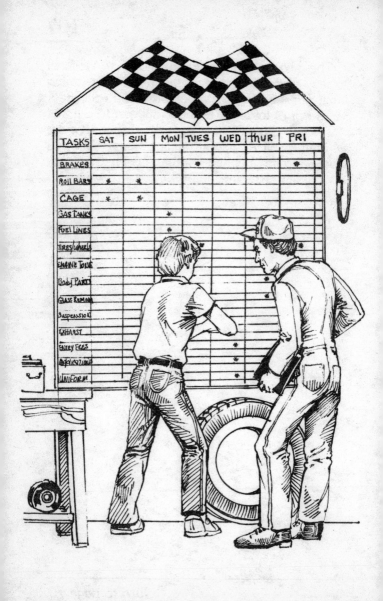

The next three hours go by quickly. You love all aspects of mechanics, from fussing with the timing chains to working on the carburetors.

There is a lot to do and you suggest to Bill that the two of you should make up a chart and put it up on the wall. At first Bill balks, because Mike was always big on "being organized." Bill had real talent with anything mechanical, but it was Mike who knew what to do and when.

Turn to page 75.

108

You take a break for a few days, turning toward algebra and biology, both tough subjects. Your exams will probably be really hard, and you need to study.

When your exams are over, you go back to your investigation. Bill is so depressed that he offers little in the way of enlightenment on who set fire to his garage.

The books on arson show how to detect the source of a fire. Sure enough, the marks the fire marshal spotted were probably fueled by gasoline.

Anyone could have done it, even Bill himself. But since he had no insurance, that seems to rule him out. You can never be sure, though—people sometimes do strange things.

Turn to page 84.

Somewhere in the back of your mind, you remember a guy last year at Thunder Road who put special equipment in his car to transfer weight while the car was in motion. These "floaters" change the way the car drives, giving a definite advantage over the other cars. The rules specifically do not allow any modifications of this kind.

Bill spotted the violation. Usually ACT officials inspect the cars and pick up any illegal alterations, but another competitor can request an investigation if illegal equipment is suspected.

Bill was right. And since this was the man's second major violation in two seasons, his license was revoked.

You remember him saying, "I'll get you one day, Mazzaro. You can count on that." Somewhere at home you have all the racing programs from last season. The man's name will be in it, you're sure. If you remember correctly, it was on a Thursday night at Thunder Road. You are certain the race was the P & C Trophy Dash.

"Bill, I have to go," you announce, giving him a light slap on the shoulder. "Things will work out."

Bill nods, but he is not smiling. Insurance for an automobile garage is high, and Bill didn't carry any.

Over dinner you ask your grandfather what he thinks.

Turn to page 77.

"Well, I think . . . I mean . . . what do you think caused the fire?" you ask, your heart pounding, hoping he will say it was accidental.

"The way I figure it, somebody poured gasoline around those two walls of the building. You can see the burn marks and stains really well in about four spots." He points them out. Sure enough, there are several spots that stand out. They are about three feet in diameter, white in the middle, then really black toward the edges.

"That would indicate a plan to burn this building. We couldn't find signs of electrical shorting except for the usual stuff when a fire rips through a building. The circuit breakers don't always trip. But this case here, I'd call it arson. It seems pretty clear."

Now is the time, so you speak up. "I don't know whether or not this is important, but my friend Mike Peterson said last week after he and Bill split up that things just might get too hot for Bill Mazzaro to handle." You pause.

"Say that again," he queries.

You repeat your conversation with Mike for the fire marshal. "It probably means nothing. I'm sorry to bother you." You feel horrible. Right now you wish you had never seen Mike or Bill in your life, let alone a stock car.

Turn to page 55.

112

The sergeant and a detective usher you into a small room with a table, four chairs, and one ceiling light. They allow you one phone call. You call your grandfather and ask him to come as quickly as possible. Then they start firing questions at you. You answer them all truthfully, but they keep coming back to the breakup of Peterson and Mazzaro. You do your best to explain why you chose to work as Mike's mechanic even though Mazzaro offered you a chance to drive. It's obvious that they don't believe you when you tell them that you felt you needed more experience before you were ready to drive on your own.

"We think you were set up to fix Peterson's car. We think you were paid big money. Now come on, turn state's witness and you'll get off easy. You know it's a murder now. Peterson's dead. The officials say that wheel was rigged to come off. And you're the mechanic."

They don't let up on you. You wish your grandfather were here. You wonder what is keeping him.

Turn to page 42.

"Well, I've got to be going," you say, edging toward the door.

"Not so fast," Mike Peterson says. He is not smiling as he closes the door to the garage and locks it. Then there is a whining sound as the electric-powered overhead doors slide into place.

"What's the matter, Mike? You don't look too happy," you say, trying to make conversation. The new mechanic moves in closer to you. He is holding a large wrench.

"Let's have a little talk," the mechanic says. "We need to clear things up. Nice and tidy like always, right, Mike?"

You don't like this one bit. But it's not as if you have any say in this conversation.

The End

ABOUT THE AUTHOR

R.A. MONTGOMERY is a graduate of Williams College. He also studied in graduate programs at Yale University and New York University. After serving in a variety of administrative capacities at Williston Academy and Columbia University, he co-founded the Waitsfield Summer School in 1965. Following that, Mr. Montgomery helped found a research and development firm specializing in the development of educational programs. He worked for several years as a consultant to the Peace Corps in Washington, D.C., and West Africa. He is now both a writer and a publisher.

ABOUT THE ILLUSTRATOR

LESLIE MORRILL is a designer and illustrator whose work has won him numerous awards. He has illustrated over thirty books for children, including the Bantam Classic edition of *The Wind in the Willows.* Mr. Morrill has illustrated many books in the Skylark Choose Your Own Adventure series, including *Home in Time for Christmas, You See the Future,* and *Stranded!* He has also illustrated *Mountain Survival, Invaders of the Planet Earth, The Brilliant Dr. Wogan, Mystery of the Sacred Stones, The Perfect Planet, The First Olympics, Hurricane!,* and *Inca Gold* in the Choose Your Own Adventure series. Mr. Morrill also illustrated both Super Adventure books, *Journey to the Year 3000* and *Danger Zones.*

Choosy Kids Choose

CHOOSE YOUR OWN ADVENTURE ®

CHOOSE YOUR OWN ADVENTURE ®

Bantam Books, Dept. AV6, 414 East Golf Road, Des Plaines, IL 60016

Please send me the items I have checked above. I am enclosing $_____ (please add $2.00 to cover postage and handling). Send check or money order, no cash or C.O.D.s please.

Mr/Ms _____

Address _____

City/State _____ Zip_____

Please allow four to six weeks for delivery.
Prices and availability subject to change without notice.

CHOOSE YOUR OWN ADVENTURE ®

Bantam Books, Dept. AV, 414 East Golf Road, Des Plaines, IL 60016

Please send me the items I have checked above. I am enclosing $_____ (please add $2.00 to cover postage and handling). Send check or money order, no cash or C.O.D.s please.

Mr/Ms _____

Address _____

City/State _____ Zip_____

AV–2/90

Please allow four to six weeks for delivery.
Prices and availability subject to change without notice.